Hello, Family Members,

Learning to read is one of the most important accomplishments of early childhood. **Hello Reader!** books are designed to help children become skilled readers who like to read. Beginning readers learn to read by remembering frequently used words like "the," "is," and "and"; by using phonics skills to decode new words; and by interpreting picture and text clues. These books provide both the stories children enjoy and the structure they need to read fluently and independently. Here are suggestions for helping your child *before*, *during*, and *after* reading:

Before

- Look at the cover and pictures and have your child predict what the story is about.
- Read the story to your child.
- Encourage your child to chime in with familiar words and phrases.
- Echo read with your child by reading a line first and having your child read it after you do.

During

- Have your child think about a word he or she does not recognize right away. Provide hints such as "Let's see if we know the sounds" and "Have we read other words like this one?"
- Encourage your child to use phonics skills to sound out new words.
- Provide the word for your child when more assistance is needed so that he or she does not struggle and the experience of reading with you is a positive one.
- Encourage your child to have fun by reading with a lot of expression . . . like an actor!

After

- Have your child keep lists of interesting and favorite words.
- Encourage your child to read the books over and over again. Have him or her read to brothers, sisters, grandparents, and even teddy bears. Repeated readings develop confidence in young readers.
- Talk about the stories. Ask and answer questions. Share ideas about the funniest and most interesting characters and events in the stories.

I do hope that you and your child enjoy this book.

—Francie Alexander
Reading Specialist,
Scholastic's Learning Ventures

For my son,
Robert Martin Staenberg,
the best gift a mother could have
—B.S.

For my good buddies,
Courtney, Tyler, and Bill,
and in memory of Lisa Clough,
a wonderful friend
and fellow mama bear
—K.B.

Text copyright © 1999 by Bonnie Staenberg.
Illustrations copyright © 1999 by Katy Bratun.
All rights reserved. Published by Scholastic Inc.
SCHOLASTIC, HELLO READER!, CARTWHEEL BOOKS
and associated logos are trademarks and/or registered
trademarks of Scholastic Inc.

Library of Congress Cataloging-in-Publication Data

Staenberg, Bonnie.
     A present for Mama Bear / by Bonnie Staenberg; illustrated by Katy Bratun.
     p. cm. — (Hello reader! Level 3)
     "Cartwheel books."
     Summary: Although he makes a mess trying to get a special present for his mother's birthday, Edgar Bear finally discovers just what she wants.
     ISBN 0-590-28154-2
     [1. Bears—Fiction. 2. Gifts—Fiction 3. Mother and son—Fiction.]
     I. Bratun, Katy, ill. II. Title. III. Series.
     PZ7.S7759Pr 1999
     [E]—dc21   98-29848
                                                             CIP
                                                             AC
12 11 10 9 8 7 6 5 4 3 2   9/9 0/0 01 02 03 04
                    Printed in the U.S.A.   24
                 First printing, April 1999

A Present for Mama Bear

by Bonnie Staenberg
Illustrated by Katy Bratun

Hello Reader! — Level 3

SCHOLASTIC INC.

Cartwheel
·B·O·O·K·S·®

New York   Toronto   London   Auckland   Sydney

Edgar Bear wanted to give
his mama a very special present
for her birthday. He wanted
to give her the best present in
the world.

"Maybe I will give her flowers," thought Edgar Bear.

So he went outside to find the prettiest flowers that grew there.

It was cloudy outside.
Edgar Bear saw some beautiful
daisies, but before he had time
to pick them, it started to rain.

Edgar Bear got all wet.

Soon he was covered in mud.

And he was cold.

"Maybe flowers are not the best present for Mama after all," he said to himself.

As he walked home, he thought and thought.

Then he had an idea.

So Edgar Bear tiptoed
up to his room and took
out his brushes and paints.

He made a picture of his house.
Then he made a picture of his
friend Alligator. And a picture
of his mama.

He was already covered with
mud, and now he had paint all
over himself, too.

When he was finished making pictures, Edgar Bear still wasn't happy.

"The pictures are pretty, but maybe they are not the best present for my mama," he said to himself.

Edgar Bear sat on the bed.

He thought and thought
and thought.

Then he had an idea.

"I will bake a cake. That will
be the best present of all."

So Edgar Bear opened the kitchen
cupboards. He saw the flour and
sugar and baking soda.

"I will mix them all together.
Then I will cook them," he thought.
"That will taste good."

When Edgar Bear reached for the
sugar box, it slipped off the shelf and
out came the sugar onto the floor.

"Oh, dear," thought Edgar Bear.
Now the sugar was ruined.

But then he smiled.

"The flour is still good," he thought.

He reached up to get the flour, but it fell onto the counter. The kitchen was a mess.

Edgar Bear was covered with mud, and paint, and now flour. He began to cry.

His mama heard the noise and came into the kitchen.

"What's this, Edgar Bear? What have you been doing?"

Edgar Bear cried even louder.

His mama picked him up in her arms.

"There, there, there," she said. "I know you're a good bear. But how did you get so dirty?"

Edgar Bear stopped crying. He told her about the cake.

Then he told her about the pictures...

and the daisies and the rain.

"Now I don't have a birthday present for you," he said with a big, sad sigh.

His mama was quiet for a minute.
Then she said, "I know what you can
give me. It will be the best present in
the world."

Edgar Bear perked up.

"What I'd like for my birthday," said his mama, "is a clean Edgar Bear."

And that is what she got.